JPIC Yum
Yum, Hyewo  W9-BHY-985
Puddle WITHDRAWN

$16.99
ocn905851230
First edition.

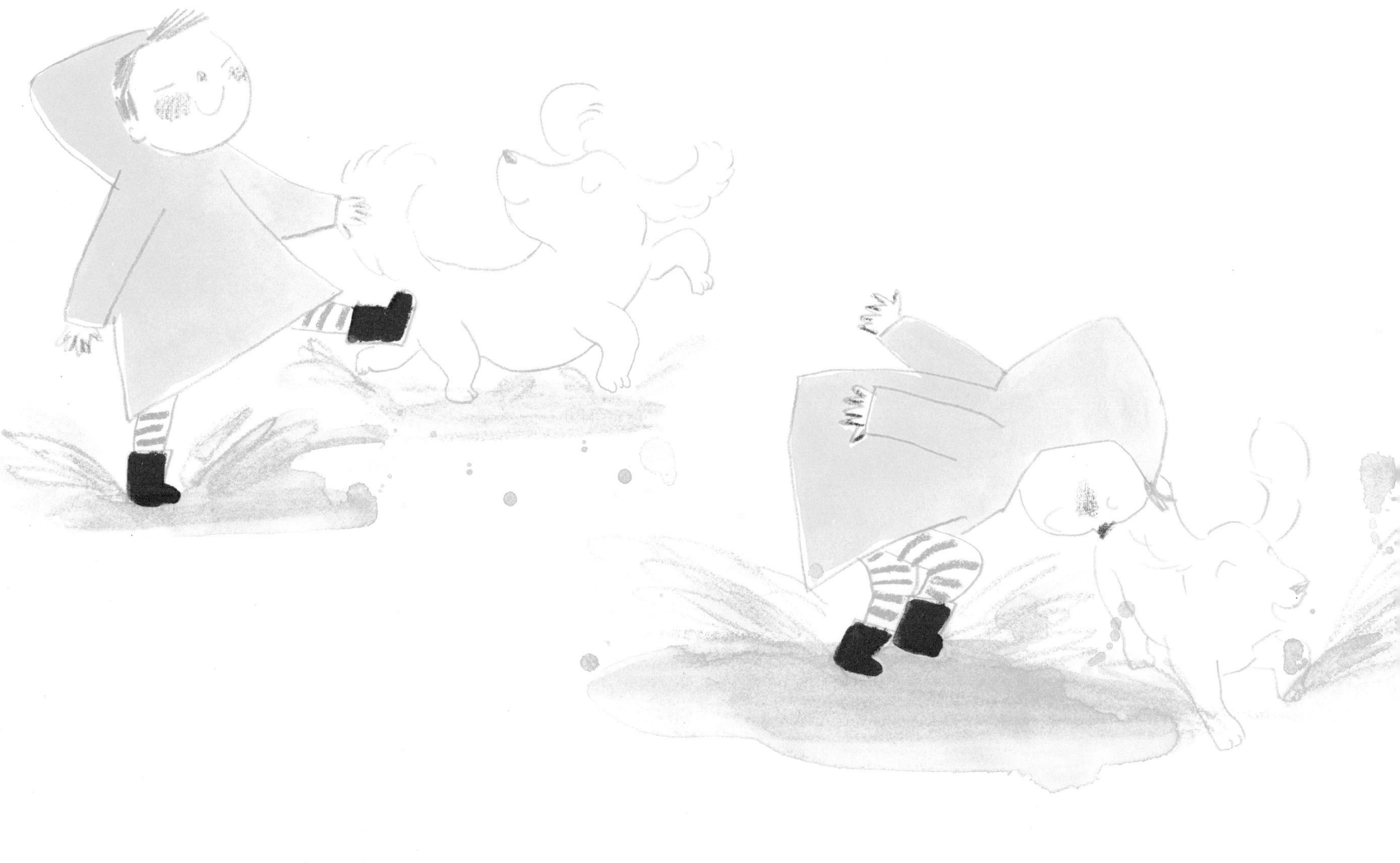

This is fun!
Can we go for a real walk?

Why not?
We have raincoats, rain boots,
and umbrellas.

Don't get mad!
It's just a picture,
you know.

Don't do that, Billy.
Mom!

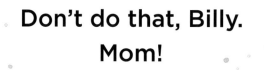

Mom, it's just a picture.
Don't get mad.

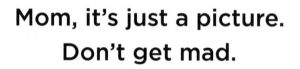

I said not to go in there.
Now you're all wet,
and I am, too.

It's a

PUDDLE!

Oh, my!
What's that?

I know.
And it's very windy.
Hold the umbrella really tight!

Oh, no!
It's pouring!

Thanks, Mom!
But there's no rain!

Right. Why don't you draw the rain?

Okay!
I'm really good at this.
Look.

There!

But where are you?
I don't want to go out all alone.

Okay, I'll draw me next to you.

And draw Billy, too.

That's a tricky one.
And I don't like wet dog smell.

Mom, please.

That's my blue umbrella.
Can you draw me holding it?

Ta-da!

It's an umbrella.

NO.
I don't want to!
I'll never draw!

Don't be so grumpy.
We can have fun at home.
Do you want to draw?

There's nothing to do.
Nothing!
I can't go to the playground.
I can't play soccer.
I can't ride my bike!

I hate rainy days.

Farrar Straus Giroux Books for Young Readers
175 Fifth Avenue, New York 10010

Copyright © 2016 by Hyewon Yum
All rights reserved
Color separations by Bright Arts
Printed in China by RR Donnelley Asia Printing Solutions Ltd.,
Dongguan City, Guangdong Province
Designed by Roberta Pressel
First edition, 2016
10 9 8 7 6 5 4 3 2

mackids.com

Library of Congress Cataloging-in-Publication Data

Yum, Hyewon.
    Puddle / Hyewon Yum. — First edition.
        pages   cm
    Summary: "A mother and son use their imagination to have fun on a rainy day"—Provided
by publisher.
    ISBN 978-0-374-31695-2 (hardback)
    [1. Mothers and sons—Fiction.   2. Rain and rainfall—Fiction.   3. Imagination—Fiction.]
    I. Title.

PZ7.Y89656Pu 2016
[E]—dc23
                                                                              2015005288

Farrar Straus Giroux Books for Young Readers may be purchased for business or promotional
use. For information on bulk purchases please contact Macmillan Corporate and Premium Sales
Department at (800) 221-7945 x5442 or by email at specialmarkets@macmillan.com.

puddle

Hyewon Yum

FARRAR STRAUS GIROUX • New York